Heart of Rebbica

ATIKSH CHOUDHARY

अंजुमन प्रकाशन

Title : Heart of Rebbica
Author : Atiksh Choudhary

Published By-
Anjuman Prakashan
942, Mutthiganj, Prayagraj, 211003
www.anjumanpublication.com
anjumanprakashan@gmail.com

Printed and bound in India.
Paperback, First published by Anjuman Prakashan in 2022
ISBN : 978-93-91531-77-5
Copyright © 2022 Atiksh Choudhary
Printing rights reserved : Anjuman Prakashan 2022
Cover & Typeset by Anjuman Prakashan

Price in india: 125/-

Dedication

To my Ma and Dr Papa. You are not only my bestest friends but also you have always been my greatest teachers. I just want to let you know how much I love both of you and care about you.

Acknowledgement–

Many thanks to my elders Charan Singh Dalal Mama Ji, Puneet Uncle, Lokesh Mama Ji, Sourav Uncle and lots of love to my brothers Mitul and Jasith.

(Author Signature)

CONTENT

Chapter- 1
Journey to the Strange Country

Bruce drank milk, and Rosie too; they asked mother, "can we go to play outside?" "Yes" said mother. After playing outside till 6:00, walking on the path till home, they suddenly fell into a bottomless pit. Aah! cried Rosie as she hit her leg on a rock.

They suddenly came into a country named Rebbica.

"What kind of place is this?" said Rosie.

"It's Rebbica," a voice came from behind.

It was an elf standing behind them. "Who are you? What is your name?' asked Bruce.

"I am Robert, an elf," said Robert.

There was magic all around the country. Elephants were as small as mice; butterflies were as big as an airplane. There were dragons, trolls, goblins, unicorns, woofers, and hidebehinds.

Rosie and Bruce were trembling with fear as they saw a dragon flying over them, but suddenly the dragon fell. A troll hit it, and the troll and his army took the dragon to the forest. An eagle suddenly swooped on one of the trolls, ate him, and kidded the others. The eagle wept for some time and then healed the dragon. As the dragon recovered, it again took fright.

Heart of Rebbica

Robert took the kids to his home; his wife and children sat, and his wife arranged dinner. Bruce ate roasted chicken, and Rosie ate rice. Then they slept. They heard a strange sound: Robert's friend Shimaro, the trainer.

It was morning. Robert and his kids woke up early, and Bruce awakened his sister. She woke up and ate food, but suddenly Shimaro came there and said, "If you want to go out from this country, Bruce and Rosie, then you have to find out the Heart of Rebbica and give it to the queen of Rebbica."

They said, "okay! We will try."

After having breakfast, they again started their Journey.

On the way, they found "Samouria City" carved on a tree, and after entering the city they saw something

Rosie

Bruce

strange, two birds were fighting with two small swords. Bruce said, "Stupid!" Inside the city, they were suddenly surrounded by two ninjas named Brasmer and Copretino.

The ninjas said, "Who are you, and why have you come to our city."

Bruce said, "I am Bruce, and this is my sister Rosie."

Then Brasmer said, "oh, so you are visitors."

Rosie said, "No, no, we want to find the Heart of Rebbica." Then they again continued their journey. By luck, they were allowed by a woman to enter her house. There they got food and a place to sleep.

They were about to leave in the morning after breakfast, but suddenly

Heart of Rebbica

Pobert

the woman called them back and gifted them two unicorns. Sitting on the unicorns, they traveled far and heard a sound. The unicorns started to tremble with fear as they listened to that sound, and their horns began to glow; and suddenly, two sharp swords landed in front of the kids. Still, a man came there, he was the great hunter Mastefia, and the sound came from his whistle. Then Bruce said, "Oh, so that's why the unicorns gave us these swords," and just then, Bruce lifted one of the swords and attached the hunter, but luckily the attack only affected Mastefia's whistle. Still, in the second attack, Mastefia died because Bruce sliced his head from his body and continued their Journey.

They were scared, but Bruce said, "Oh, Rosie, don't be so scared; we have two powerful unicorns." Then suddenly, the horns of the unicorns began to glow, and a bright flash appeared, and then all of a sudden, the unicorns grew wings.

One unicorn said, "Dear kids, we are made to help someone out from a problem, and you are the one to seek our help, so sit on our backs."

They both sat on each unicorn and flew away; on the way, they saw a river, and the unicorns dived straight into the river, and then Rosie said, "It's God's mercy on us that we found a river, I have not taken a shower from last two days." After taking a shower, they drove themselves with the help of the unicorns and flew away.

On their journey, they were attacked by a group of goblins, but to save the kids, the unicorn started to blow their horns and threw fire at the goblins; after a few minutes, all the goblins were lying dead, and they flew away on their way.

* * *

Shimaro

Braemar

coperline

Chapter- 2
Dry Steps

Rosie and Bruce slept on the unicorns the whole night and found themselves flying above a desert in the morning.

Bruce said, "The weather here is unbearable. I think we should go down and make a shelter ". Then they went down to stay there for some time, and suddenly they were overtaken by a horse covered in flames, saying, "Welcome to the great Obamia desert, here you will find many kinds of creatures."

Suddenly one of the unicorns

interrupted between them, "Oh, hi Grunter, nice to see you, old champ!." And then Grunter said, "Oh, sorry, Panter, I did not notice you, and yes, you did not tell me that another unicorn is with you, is he your friend?."

Panter said," Yes, he is my friend, and his name is Crob, and he is shy to talk."

Then they went with Grunter to his home; on their way to Grunter's home, they met a gigantic crab and a man with a hubble-bubble in his bag.

They both asked, "who are you?"

Bruce said, "Um… well, we are new to this desert, and my name is Bruce, and this is my sister Rosie, and these are our friend's Ratter, Grunter, and Crob."

 Heart of Rebbica

"Oh! Mr. New…..I mean, Mr. Bruce, can you and your friends have hubble-bubble with us?" "No, no need of it," said Rosie, and then the man said," I think I forgot something." He went into deep thoughts, and after some time, he said, "Oh, yes, I found it! I forgot to tell you my name…. My name is Braly, and this is my brother Crabenter, he has been cursed by a witch to look like a crab, and only one thing can make him well like before, which is to kill the Witch."

Rosie went pale white and said, "How will you kill her?"

The man said, "By the potion of the Great Grandferd wizard."

"We are off on a journey to Grandferd," said Braly.

Heart of Rebbica

"Okay! But do you know someone named Bruce?" Bruce asked "Oh yes, he was my great-great-great-grandfather," Braly replied.

The kids were shocked to listen to this; then Rosie asked, "Oh, but just answer me that do you know someone named Rosie?" "No, but I know that this is you and your friend's last day in this world; I am not Braly but the witch, and he is not my brother Crabenter but my dearest pet bird; his name is Kitash, ha ha ha ha…." He screamed, and they both transformed into their evil form. Grandfield was seeing everything from the sky, and he clapped three times and chanted, "Witchado flamo!" Suddenly, giant balls of fire started to attack the Witch and her pet Kitash.

The Witch screamed, "Nooo, Grandferd came here also; let's go from here, Kitash." They vanished from there, then Grandferd appeared in front of the siblings and said, "My dear kids, sorry to bother you, the witch was my evil sister Ferina, and I am going to grant you each a boon; tell me what do you want?"

Bruce said, "Can you grant me that I can not be burnt by fire." And Rosie asked, "Grant me the ability to fly."

It was Grunter, Panter, and Crob's chance for a boon, but they denied it, and Grandferd disappeared from there, and they again started their Journey to Grunter's home. Bruce sat on Grunter because he was granted a boon to not burn by fire, and Rosie flew to Grunter's home. After reaching home, his wife had made delicious food for the kids, but Bruce suddenly screamed and said, "Oh no! Rosie, we forgot to ask the wizard to let us get out of this country." Rosie also said, "Oh no!"

* * *

Eerina

Chapter- 3
On the Journey again

After waking up and having breakfast in the morning, the kids packed up some food that Grunter's wife gave them and sat on unicorns to start their Journey again, but the unicorns denied it. The kids were shocked to hear this, but suddenly something strange happened. Winds began to blow in black and collected in the form of a small tornado, and at last, the tornado was over, but after that, two baby dragons appeared there, and while watching them, Rosie said, "Awwww, they are so cute. Should we tame them?"

"Okay, why not." Said Bruce.

After observing them for some time, Grunter said, "Children remember, these are foodie pilasco dragons; whoever gives them food to eat for the first time they consider him as their master, so you both take this meat and feed them." So they went to feed the dragons. The dragons ate food steadily, and alas! They grew as big as a mountain; they bowed before Bruce and Rosie, and both the kids said, "Okay, but now they are not adorable as before. Should we sit on them and continue our journey?"

"Go go; you should; they mean no harm to you guys; you are their master." And then the kids bid goodbye to everyone and sat on the dragons, and

          Heart of Rebbica

the dragons flew, as the dragons flew and they gave themselves a boost while flying, and yes, it was a funny sight because they were throwing poop from their bums.

After flying the whole night they reached a city, it was full of future machines, highly technical equipment, there were no animals at all. The kids were amazed to see this and said, "What an amazing place it is! Let's go down for some time?"

As they went down, they found a man and asked him, "What is this place? Where is it located?"

"It is Uda in the future Rebbica and its miles under the Bermuda Triangle," answered the man.

The kids were shocked to hear that they were under Bermuda Triangle.

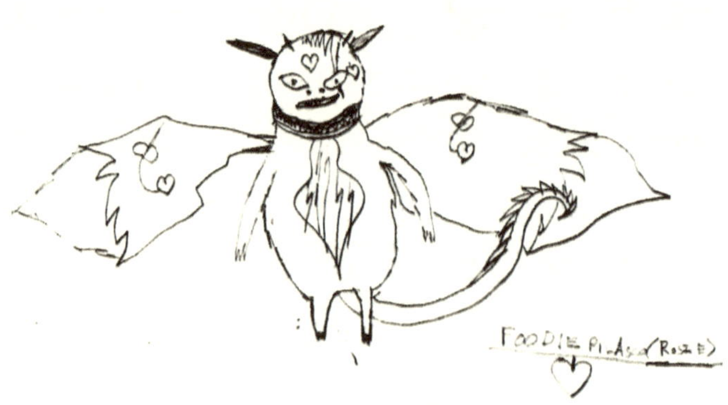
FOODIE PLeAse (RosIE)

"Is there any way to get out from here?" asked the kids.

"Yes, there are many ways to get out from here, but I don't know because all the people of the city and I are not of Rebbica; I will tell you the whole story. We were on a casino ship, and I was the ship's captain. We were sailing near Bermuda Triangle, and the next day we didn't notice that we came so much near the Bermuda Triangle that it sucked us, but we were lucky because we landed straight on a mushroom kind thing, and it bounced us in Rebbica" said the man. "You mean that Rebbica is whole under water?" asked Rosie.

"Yes, my dear, you are right," said the man, but suddenly a robot eagle landed in front of the kids and said,

"How dare you talk to our master?" And came into a position to attack the kids, but the man interrupted him and said, "Stop Via, they are my friends." "Okay, master," said Via and flew away.

"Sorry, he is a little hot-headed," said the man."

"It's okay," said the kids, but after an hour or two, Bruce whispered to Rosie and said, "Rosie, I think it's not safe to stay here; let's go." "Okay," said Rosie.

The man gave them each a stick like bread, ate them and bid goodbye to the man, and flew away on their dragons.

* * *

    Heart of Rebbica

Foodie Palace (Bunny)

Heart of Rebbica

Chapter -4
The Witch again

While flying, they did not notice that they left Uda and came into witch territory where Grandferd's evil sister lived, and she saw them coming and collected a small army of witches and started to launch rockets. The rockets flew into the air and exploded in red color. Suddenly a witch came flying with a missile, but before she could attack, Bruce's dragon blew flame at the Witch; the Witch died, but others were still alive, and the dragons were about to strike other witches, but suddenly a man wearing high – tech suit came flying on a robot eagle. "Via and that man from Uda are coming to help us?" Screamed Bruce; the man came near and said, "Don't call me man, my name is Captain Frank" while saying he took a long gun and shot all the witches except Ferina because she flew away with Kitash.

"Thank you for saving our lives, Mr. Frank," said Rosie. "Welcome, my dear child, and yes, take these gadgets shield maker, spy warp, jetpacks, special suits, auto guns, and special unlimited grenade bag," said Mr. Frank.

* * *

Mr. Frank
Via

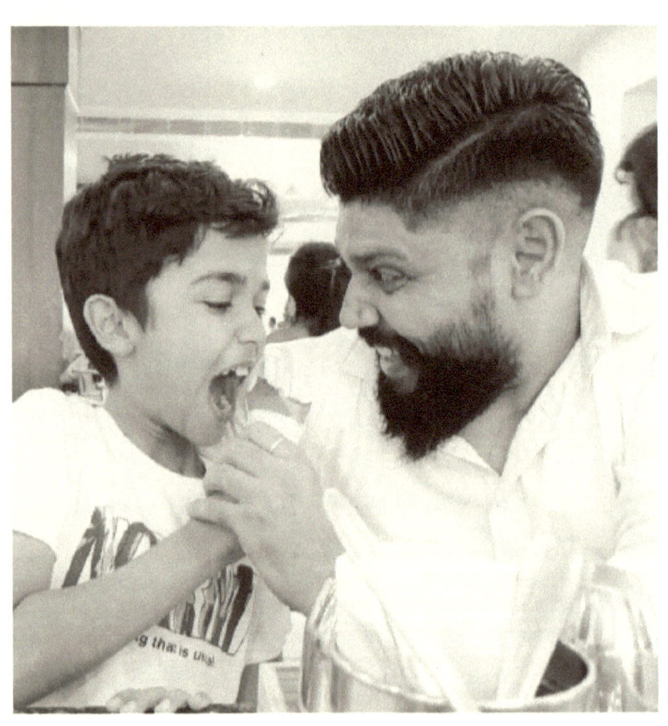

Chapter- 5
Gadget Trouble

After crossing Witch territory, the kids landed down to take a rest. At night they didn't sleep; Rosie sat under a tree and started to carve something on the sand with a stick, and Bruce began to see the gadgets; he took the grenade bag and took out a grenade on the tree under which Rosie was sitting. The tree turned into a large stone and was about to fall on Rosie, but before it could fall, Bruce created a shield around Rosie with the help of the shield maker. The stone broke into pieces when it touched the protection;

after that, Bruce removed the guard from there by pressing a button on the shield maker and said to Rosie, "Now, let's try these special suits and jetpacks."

"Okay," said Rosie, and they both clicked a button on their suits. The suits opened, and the kids wore them; they also hung the jetpacks on their shoulders like a school bag, pressed the button on their jetpacks, and flew. While flying, they came to their dragons and told them to continue the Journey, so both dragons flew with the kids, they all dived in the air happily, but soon the happiness had gone because a giant troll attacked them. He threw big stones at the kids, but they were wearing suits, so the rocks were not able to hurt them; then Bruce suddenly threw one grenade from the

          Heart of Rebbica

grenade bag; the grenade went flying and landed near the troll, it exploded, and the troll got froze for some time. The kids were about to go away from there, but the troll deferred himself, he was more aggressive than earlier and was about to attack Bruce, but his dragon saw this and grabbed the troll by the neck and killed him. Bruce patted his dragon on the head when he saw the dead troll. They did not want to stay there anymore, so they flew away; while flying, Rosie said to Bruce, "Bruce, can we spy on that little bird with the help of a spy wasp?"

"Okay," said Bruce and switched on the wasp. It flew down to the bird slowly and followed it, Bruce and Rosie saw it on a small screen, but suddenly there was no signal on the screen. Then they heard a loud bang, and by that sudden bang, Bruce accidentally dropped the gadgets except for the suits and jetpacks because they were wearing them, and the other devices broke. Rosie said, "Oh no! all the other gadgets are broken; now we are only left with these jetpacks and suits and what we will do from these, so let's drop these also." "Yes, you are right, Rosie, so 3,2 and 1…go!" said Bruce, dropping it.

* * *

Chapter-6
The Spirit Land

After the gadgets broke, the kids sadly continued their Journey. On their journey, they heard a rustling sound and spotted a blue figure, but it soon disappeared.

"What was that?" asked Bruce.

"Don't know," said Rosie, and she saw a book lying near a tree and picked it up. It was written "don't touch" on the book, but Rosie still picked it up, and suddenly the blue figure appeared before them and said, "How dare you touch the book! I Nova, the spirit queen of dragons, will kill you."

" No, no! your highness, don't kill us; we didn't know it," said Rosie. Are you blind? Can't you even read anything? Okay! If you don't know, I will let you free but only on one condition, that press the blue-colored gem on the book. Rosie quickly pressed it, and Nora suddenly transformed into a beautiful woman and vanished away from there; after going a little far, they saw many other spirits, one of the spirits flew in front of them and said, "welcome to the Spirit land."

"What, the spirit land!" said Bruce.

"Yes, spirit land," said the spirit.

There were many old, broken houses and bungalows. "These are our houses," said the spirit. "What is your name, dear spirit," asked Bruce. " It's Moco, my dear, and my kids are Max,

                              Heart of Rebbica

Harry, and Mary." Harry was playing with small stones and throwing them here and there, whereas Mary and Max were learning to fly, falling repeatedly.

"Wow! What a place," said Rosie.

"Do you want to play with me?" asked Harry.

"Yes, why not" replied Rosie and Bruce agreed too, and they started to play hide-seek with Harry. They played till 8 pm in the night, then ate food and slept; they woke up around 7 am, took a shower, ate food, and set off on their Journey. Harry was feeling anxious where the kids were gone, so he also followed them; when Harry was following the kid, Bruce suddenly slipped from his flying dragon and fell down the sky, Harry saw this and quickly rushed to catch him, and finally, he caught him.

"Harry! How you come here?" Said Bruce.

"I was following you guys," explained Harry.

"Okay, but now go away from here!" scolded Bruce.

"He saved your life, and you are scolding him, Bruce. Don't you think we should go with Harry to his home for one more night and play with him," said Rosie.

"Sorry for scolding Harry and Rosie, you are saying the right thing; we can go to Harry's home to play and spend one more night there," said Bruce. So they went to Harry's home and played till night after that they slept. In the morning, they took a shower, ate food, and flew on their dragons; they entered the portal by mistake and came to Uda again; they were confused and thought about how they came to Uda. Rosie suddenly spotted a portal and said, "I think we come here through that portal; we should try to enter it again."

"Yes, Rosie, we should try to enter that portal." Replied Bruce; they entered the portal and reached near Robert's house; like this, they, again and again, entered the portal and finally arrived. After getting out of the portal, they continued their Journey to the Heart of Rebbica, and they saw some flying mice, zombies, and a few walking snakes. They were scared when they saw them. "What are these scary-looking weird creatures," said Rosie.

"These are homo flops," Said Bruce.

"Bruce! How do you know this?" asked Rosie.

"Oh! This I read from a book which Harry secretly gave me." Replied Bruce.

"Okay, Bruce, but I think we forgot something," said Rosie. "What we forgot, Rosie," asked Bruce.

"We forgot that we have powers which we granted by Grandferd that day, he gave me the ability to fly, and you were granted that you can't ever be burnt by fire," replied Rosie.

"Oh yes, I remember it," said Bruce, and they tried their powers.

It was working! Rosie flew up to the sky, and Bruce stood in front of the dragons releasing fire.

 Heart of Rebbica

"Wow! It's enjoyable," said Bruce.

"Bruce, I think you should try to release fire by your hands?" said Rosie. "No, I can't do it, Rosie," replied Bruce.

"Why?" asked Rosie.

"Because I am only granted that I can't be burnt by fire," replied Bruce. "Okay," said Rosie.

"But Rosie, I think you can do this," said Bruce.

"What I can do, Bruce?" asked Rosie.

"You can let your dragonfly alone and by yourself," replied Bruce. "Yes, I can do this," said Rosie.

So Bruce sat on his dragon, and Rosie started to fly; while flying, they saw another dragon on which a man was sitting. They went closer to him, but he wore a mask and had a bow and a sword. "Cool!" said Bruce.

"I want to see his face one time," said Rosie.

"So let's ask him," replied Bruce.

They went near him and asked, "Can you please remove your mask? We want to see your face."

"Rosie and Bruce! How you are here?" asked the man. "How you know our names! Anyways we came here accidentally through a pit," replied Rosie.

The man removed his mask; to their surprise, it was their father. "Father, how are you here? You were dead on my 8th birthday, and now I am eleven, and Rosie is twelve," asked Bruce.

"That day, I was about to die in that

   Heart of Rebbica

accident, but Grandferd saved me and told me to be the soldier of the Queen of Rebbica," Replied Father. "So, father do you know the way to the heart of Rebbica?" asked Rossie. "Yes, I know, "replied father but suddenly changed and said "No" again and again, but at last, he agreed that he knew the way to the heart of Rebbica.

* * *

Chapter 7
Pet selection

"Okay, so let's start," said father.

"Okay," said both the kids, and they flew up.

While flying, they were talking, "Do you know, kids, my sword has such a power that if I throw it, it comes back," said father. "Really! can you show us?" asked Bruce.

"Ok," replied father, and he threw the sword, which returned. "Father, do you have any pet?" asked Rosie.

"Yes, I have pets," replied father.

"Can you show us?" asked Rosie.

"Yes, see, here is my small ice, " said father taking out a small animal from his bag; it was a small fox-like animal. "And, the second pet is this dragon," said father.

"Father, we also need a pet?" asked Rosie.

"Yes, father," said Bruce.

"Okay, but for that, you have to find animals in the jungle; I will help you in that," answered father, and they landed in the jungle over which they were flying and started to find animals to tame. Bruce soon caught a tiny white mouse-like animal, and Rosie caught a bat, and their father saw their animal species and said, "Rosie, you caught a wolf bat, and Bruce, you caught a lion mouse, take care of these pets. These will help you any time you are in trouble.

"Okay, Dad," replied the kids.

"Okay, now sit on your dragons and start," said dad.

"Ok," replied the kids, and they all flew away.

* * *

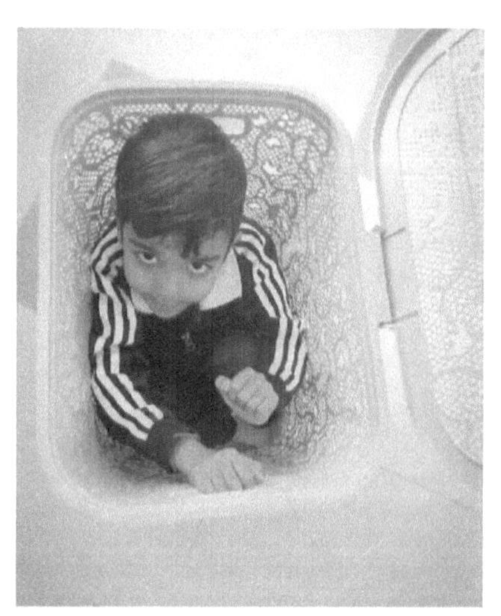

Heart of Rebbica

Chapter 8

On Rabbican journey

While flying, they were talking about Ferina.

Dad said, "Ferina is very cruel and dangerous, one time, she attacked me, and I was about to die, but at that time, a man flying on a dragon shooted Ferina. She saved herself but was scared and ran away from me."

"She attacked us also once in the Obamia desert and Witch territory. In Obamia desert, Grandferd saved us, and in Witch territory, a man saved us," replied kids.

Suddenly the sky was getting red, and just then, Ferina came from the sky; Bruce took his father's sword and sliced Ferina's head, and their sword returned.

They flew away, and dad said, "I forgot the way. I think we should ask someone" just then, Bruce saw a man flying on a dragon, and they asked him where the way to the heart of Rebbica was?

"Yes, I know. Can you see that hill? There are three hills, one after one. On the first one, you have to fight a large army of wolves, and on the second one, you have to fight with firemen, and on the third one, there is the heart of Rebbica, but here also you have to fight an army, but I don't know that in the last one whom you have to fight with" answered the man.

"Ok," replied Bruce and Rosie. They flew to the first hill and reached there. It was too big, and there was indeed a large army of wolves. They burned all wolves with the help of their dragons; then, they flew to the fire trolls next hill. It was far, and they reached there in 1–2 hours. After entering the mountain and to their amazement, their dragon changed form; they sprang water on all the fire trolls and were dead in no time. They started flying to the third one. While passing, they were surrounded by gnomes flying on swoopers. One was flying too near to Bruce; he kicked the gnome. It fell and died, Bruce caught the fwooper and fed it. Now the fwooper was his! Fwooper told all his friends to leave the gnomes and kill them. The fwoopers flew straight up, and the gnomes fell and died. They thought all the gnomes were finished but the king of gnomes was still alive. He came and took out his sword and challenged them. They accepted his challenge and started to fight. First, the gnome threw his sword, but they saved themselves from his attack; then, their dad threw his sword. The blade did not hit the gnome and returned; just then, the gnome did some magic and transformed into a ninja and threw ninja stars at them. They saved themselves from it, then quickly, dad threw his sword at the gnome. Now the blade hit the gnome, and he died, then their dad jumped from his dragon and started spinning his sword to fly. He went slowly down, and after some time, he came up and said, "I took the magic power of the

Heart of Rebbica

gnome. Can I show it to you?" "Yes, replied the kids, then dad threw a ball of fire and controlled it, and he took it on the right side and exploded, then he made a ball of water, froze it, and threw it. It went straight down and broke.

"Do you want some powers of magic? I have powers of wind, fire, water, forest, and to transform. You can take any two from these," asked dad.

"I will take transforming and fire," replied Bruce.

"I will take wind and water," said Rosie.

"Okay, but I have all the powers since it can't go from my body; I am just sharing you," replied dad.

"Ok," said the kids.

Bruce said, "See, I can become a dragon," and transformed into a dragon.

"Wow," said Rosie.

Bruce transformed into a natural form. Now it was evening, the sky was a little dark, but still, some light was visible. Suddenly an arrow went from their side; a man was coming toward them. "Who are you?" said Bruce.

"I am Max," replied the man and shot another arrow. He was flying on a red dragon; dad said, "It's a red infernape; it's dangerous species if someone tames it. This dragon gives the owner power of transforming; this dragon too can transform." Then Bruce saw behind the dragon and Max were not visible, suddenly two small

  Heart of Rebbica

blue bullets went from their side and transformed into a man and dragon. It was Max. He reshot an arrow, now the hand transformed into a bullet and again transformed back into an arrow, but Bruce's dragon burned it.

Rosie asked Max, "Why are you fighting with us?"

"Because you will have to fight me to cross my city," replied Max.

"Ok," said Rosie.

Then Max took a gun and said, "These are called demolators." We use them to shoot crawlies. They are small insects, we launch them from the demolators, and now I only have one crawler; it is an Armored wolf crawler. You will also have to find at least five crawlies and a demolater, and I will also find four crawlies.

"Ok," said Bruce, and they went down; first, they went into the city to take demolators, found a man who gave them three demolators, and then they went to find crawlies. Bruce quickly found five crawlies, then Rosie and dad found five and went again to Max. He said, "Let's go down and fight."

"Yes," said Rosie, and they all went down first. Bruce shot the crawler, it transformed into a giant monster and hit Max and he died.

* * *

Chapter-9
We Found it !

So they reached the heart of Rebbica, it was in a cave, and a vast army of goblins and trolls was standing in front of it. Dragons of Rosie and Bruce's kidded them quickly, and their father was surprised by this; and he asked them, "Are these dragons Foodie Pilasco?"

"Yes," replied the children.

Their father was shocked to listen to this and said, "Why didn't you tell me?"

"Because you did not ask," replied

Bruce.

"Okay, but you know that Foodie Pilasco is the strongest dragon breed." Said their father.

"No, we did not know," replied Rosie, and then they quickly took the Heart of Rebbica.

It was a large green stone with a heart in between, and then they went straight to the queen's palace and gave it to her, and she said, "you have done excellent work, my dear soldier Darwin and now I want to grant you a boon. "I am not from Rebbica I am sorry that I did not tell you about it. I am from a nonmagical land called Earth, and now I want to go back to my home," replied the children's father, Darwin.

"Okay, as you wish," said the

                    Heart of Rebbica

queen, lifting the Heart of Rebbica and chanting something. Suddenly there was a bright flash, and a portal opened; all of them entered the portal.

* * *

QUEEN OF REBBICA

Chapter- 10

We are back

When they reached home, their mother was shocked to see them home; she hugged and kissed her children and was amazed to see her husband.

"How you came here?" said their mother.

"It is a very long story; we will tell you afterward. First, give us food; we are starving, " Bruce replied. "Ok," said mother.

✷ ✷ ✷

Heart of Rebbica

Dear Son,

You are the biggest ray of light in our family. May you be surrounded by all the things that make you smile. We both love you a lot, you are making us proud since you have taken your first step on the soil. Keep believing in yourself and moving ahead.

www.ingramcontent.com/pod-product-compliance
Lightning Source LLC
Chambersburg PA
CBHW020737160726
47993CB00006B/2490